My Foot Fell Asleep

Selected by
Sarah Keane

Illustrated by
Holly Hatam

Lee Aucoin, *Creative Director*
Jamey Acosta, *Senior Editor*
Heidi Fiedler, *Editor*
Produced and designed by
Denise Ryan & Associates
Illustration © Holly Hatam
Rachelle Cracchiolo, *Publisher*

Teacher Created Materials
5301 Oceanus Drive
Huntington Beach, CA 92649-1030
http://www.tcmpub.com
Paperback: ISBN: 978-1-4333-5567-7
Library Binding: ISBN: 978-1-4807-1712-1

Contents

My Foot Fell Asleep

My foot fell asleep
right inside of my shoe
from sitting around
having nothing to do.

It hadn't drank warm milk
nor tried to count sheep;
it just wasn't busy,
and fell right asleep.

Z
Z
Z

You see, in my shoe
it gets lonely and boring,
which made my foot sleepy,
and soon it was snoring.

My foot snored so loudly
my shoe began flapping.
But it didn't notice—
it kept right on napping!

Z Z Z Z Z

It slept through the morning
and most of the day,
despite that my other foot
wanted to play.
It took a siesta.
It slumbered inert.
It nodded through dinner.
It dozed through dessert.

Now I'm in my bed
and I've been up all night.
I'm trying to sleep,
although try as I might,
my foot slept all day
(what a foolish mistake!)
now I can't fall asleep
'cause my foot's wide awake!

Kenn Nesbitt

Heather Potts

Heather Potts is awfully thin.
She's lighter than a feather,
Which makes her interesting to watch
In very windy weather.

Cynthia Rider

Home Haircut

Nellie, cutting Johnnie's hair,
Was taking insufficient care;
She turned to hear what someone said,
And found that she'd cut off his head!
She smiled, "I know what to do."
And stuck it on again with glue.

John Cuncliffe

Frankenstein's Monster World Tour

I left my heart in San Francisco,
My torso in Nepal,
My arms in Valparaiso
And my legs in Montreal.

I lost my ears in New York City
And in Trinidad, my hair.
Lost my memory in. . .
(Now where was it I lost my memory?)
Oh, I can't remember where.

And if that wasn't bad enough
I think I'm losing my voice. . .

Colin McNaughton

My Mouth

stays shut
but
food just
finds
a way
my tongue says
we are
full today
but
teeth just
grin
and
say
come in.
I am always hungry.

Arnold Adoff

Oodles of Noodles

I love noodles. Give me oodles.
Make a mound up to the sun.
Noodles are my favorite foodles.
I eat noodles by the ton.

Lucia and James L. Hynes Jr.

The Sidewalk Racer
Or
On The Skateboard

Skimming
an asphalt sea
I swerve, I curve, I
sway; I speed to whirring
sound an inch above the
ground; I'm the sailor
and the sail, I'm the
driver and the wheel
I'm the one and only
single engine
human auto
mobile.

Lillian Morrison

sk8

I Can Fly

I can fly, of course
Very low,
Not fast,
Rather slow.
I spread my arms
Like wings,
Lean on the wind,
And my body zings
About.
Nothing showy—
A few loops
And turns—
But for the most
Part,
I just coast.

However,
Since people are prone
To talk about
It,
I generally prefer,
Unless I am alone,
Just to walk about.

Felice Holman

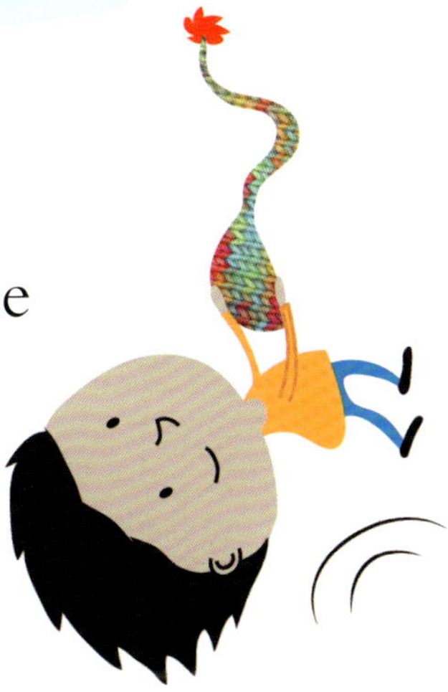

I FEEL SICK

Set off before dawn, sick,
    Feeling very, yawn, sick,
Wish I'd not been born, sick,
    I FEEL SICK!

Is it very far, sick,
    Ate a chocolate bar, sick,
Feeling very carsick,
    I FEEL SICK!

Corner of my eye, sick,
Trees are flashing by, sick,
Wish that I could die, sick,
I FEEL SICK!

Dad says "look ahead," sick,
Wish that I was dead, sick,
Take me home to bed, sick.
I FEEL SICK!

Queasy, woozy, hot, sick,
  My brother says I'm not sick,
Thanks a rotten lot, sick,
  I FEEL SICK!

Twisty, turny road, sick,
  Chocolate overload, sick,
Ready to explode, sick,
  I FEEL SICK!

Daddy, hurry up, sick,
Feel it coming up, sick,
Hic! Hiccup! Hiccup! Sick!
I'VE BEEN SICK!

P. S.

Didn't make the door, sick.
Threw up on the floor, sick.
There isn't any more sick.

I FEEL FINE!

Colin McNaughton

Mark's Fingers

I like my fingers.
They grip a ball,
Turn a page,
Break a fall,
Help whistle
A call.

Shake hands
And shoot
Rubber bands.
When candy is offered
They take enough.
They fill my pockets
With wonderful stuff,
And they always tell me
Smooth from rough.

They follow rivers

On a map,
They double over
When I rap,
They smack together
When I clap.
They button buttons,
Tie shoelaces,
Open doors to
Brand new places.
They shape and float
My paper ships,
Fasten papers to
Paper clips,
And carry ice cream
To my lips. . .

Mary O'Neill

Everybody Says

Everybody says
I look just like my mother.
Everybody says
I'm the image of Aunt Bee.
Everybody says
My nose is like my father's
But *I* want to look like ME!

Dorothy Aldis

Sources and Acknowledgments

Adoff, Arnold. "My Mouth." Originally published in *Eats*. New York: Lotrop, Lee, and Shepard Books, 1979. Reprinted by permission of Arnold Adolf.

Aldis, Dorothy. "Everybody Says." Originally published in *Here, There and Everywhere*. New York: Minton, Balch, and Company, 1936.

Cuncliffe, John. "Home Haircut." Originally published in *Standing on a Strawberry*. New York: Scholastic,1987. Reprinted by permission of Andre Deutsch, London, UK.

Hymes, Lucia and James L. Jr. "Oodles of Noodles." Originally published in *Oodles of Noodles* and Other Hymes' Rhymes. Boston: Addison-Wesley Publishing Company, 1964. Reprinted by permission of Addison-Wesley Publishing Company, Boston, USA.

McNaughton, Colin. "Frankenstein's Monster World Tour" and "I Feel Sick." Originally published in *Wish You Were Here (And I Wasn't)*. London: Walker Books, 1999. Reprinted by permission of Walker Books, London, UK.

Morrison, Lillian. "The Sidewalk Racer." Originally published in *The Sidewalk Racer and Other Poems of Sports and Action*. New York Lothrop, Lee, and Shepard Books, 1977. Reprinted by permission of Lothrop, Lee & Shepard Books (Imprint of HarperCollins) New York, USA.

Nesbitt, Kenn. "My Foot Fell Asleep." Originally published in *My Hippo Has the Hiccups and Other Poems I Totally Made Up. New York:* Sourcebooks Jabberwocky, 2009. Reprinted by permission of Sourcebooks Jabberwocky, New York, USA.

O'Neill, Mary. "Mark's Fingers." Originally published in *My Fingers Are Always Bringing Me News*. Los Angeles: International Creative Management, Incorporated, 1969. Reprinted by permission of International Creative Management, Inc. Los Angeles, USA.

Rider, Cynthia. "Heather Potts." Originally published in *Ridiculous Rhymes* picked by John Foster. London: HarperCollins, 2001. Reprinted by permission of HarperCollins, London, UK.